*For Jack Evans*

First published 2010 by
A & C Black Publishers Ltd
36 Soho Square, London, W1D 3QY

www.acblack.com
www.damianharvey.co.uk

Text copyright © 2010 Damian Harvey
Illustrations copyright © 2010 Ned Joliffe

The rights of Damian Harvey and Ned Joliffe to be identified as
the author and illustrator of this work have been asserted by them in
accordance with the Copyrights, Designs and Patents Act 1988.

ISBN 978-1-4081-1385-1

A CIP catalogue for this book is available from the British Library.

This book is produced using paper that is made from wood
grown in managed, sustainable forests. It is natural, renewable and
recyclable. The logging and manufacturing processes conform
to the environmental regulations of the country of origin.

Printed and bound in Great Britain
by CPI Cox & Wyman, Reading, RG1 8EX.

# THE MUD CRUSTS

## DIRTY DEEDS

## Damian Harvey
### Illustrated by Ned Joliffe

**A & C Black • London**

# Chapter ONE

Dark, black mud oozed between Lowbrow Mudcrust's toes and slowly covered his hairy feet.

"That feels better," he said, sitting down on a rock and having a good stretch. "It's nice to be home."

Lowbrow and his wife, Flora, had spent the morning visiting Chief Hawknose and his family in their cave near the bottom of Icecap Mountain. Visiting Chief Hawknose always put Lowbrow in a bad mood and he had grumbled all the way back home.

"Hawknose thinks he's so special," Lowbrow complained. "With his fancy cave and his perfect daughter."

"I don't know why you two can't just be friends," said Flora.

"I'm not going to be friends with that old cheat," said Lowbrow. "If I never see him again, it won't be too soon!"

"Well you *will* be seeing him again," said Flora. "He's chief of our tribe and he's married to my sister."

"*I* should be chief," grumbled Lowbrow. "My father was chief before him and I would be now, too, if old Bignose hadn't cheated in the trials."

"That was a long time ago," said Flora. "But you know, you *could* always challenge him. If you won, you would be the new chief."

Lowbrow didn't reply. He just sat there, wriggling his toes in the mud.

Flora didn't mind that her husband was not chief of the tribe. She was more interested in their home. Chief Hawknose's cave had been so nice, and Fauna, her sister, said it was easy to keep clean and tidy. But no matter what she did, *their* hut was always a muddy mess, and it made Flora cross.

"I'm fed up with living in this swamp," she grumbled. "We must find somewhere else to live."

"Somewhere *else*?" cried Lowbrow, jumping up off his rock.

"Yes!" said Flora. "Somewhere else."

"But the Mudcrusts have lived in Slimepool Swamp for years," said Lowbrow. "My father lived here. My father's father lived here and my father's father's father lived here, too."

It was true, the Mudcrusts *had* lived in the swamp for as long as anyone could remember. But Flora didn't care.

"Just because *your* family never managed to leave does not mean *we* can't," she said firmly. "I'm fed up with all this mud. It gets everywhere. It sticks to our clothes. It gets in our food. *And* it stinks."

Lowbrow normally did what his wife wanted. It meant she didn't shout at him as much. Flora could be very frightening when she shouted. But Lowbrow was determined not to move. His great-grandfather had built their hut at the edge of the swamp with his own hands, and Lowbrow was very proud of it.

"This is the Mudcrust family home," he said. "As long as this hut stands, the Mudcrusts will stay."

"The swamp is getting swampier every day," observed Flora. "I wouldn't be surprised if it sank soon."

"Nonsense!" said Lowbrow. "This hut has stood here through wind and rain, snow and hail —"

But Flora wasn't listening. She was wondering if there might be some way of getting their hut to sink into the mud even sooner. If that happened, the Mudcrusts would *have* to find somewhere else to live. Perhaps *then* they could have a nice cave like her sister and Chief Hawknose.

She wondered if Bogweed, their youngest son, would be able to help. Bogweed was a clever boy, and he was always coming up with bright ideas. She decided to look for him at once.

As Flora stepped out of the hut, a horrible smell nearly knocked her off her feet. It was as if she had walked into

a solid wall of stink, and her eyes began to water. It was the sort of smell that would stop a sabre-toothed tiger in its tracks. It smelt worse than a wet woolly mammoth. It could mean only one thing.

Fungus.

"Hello, dear," said Flora, wiping her eyes. "Have you seen your brother?"

Fungus, her eldest son, was sitting on a damp log, banging two sticks together. He'd seen Bogweed make a fire using little piles of sticks, but he couldn't quite get the hang of it himself.

"He's in the pong pit," said Fungus pulling a face.

Flora shook her head. She liked things to be nice and clean, but Bogweed went too far. He was *always* lying in the pong pit and it made him smell funny. Though it was a nicer smell than Fungus, she had to admit.

Flora set off along the path that wound its way through Slimepool Swamp, wondering how she could get Fungus to go in the pong pit. It wouldn't be easy, but it would make things much better for everyone.

14

Winter was coming and soon the Mudcrusts would be spending most of their time indoors trying to keep warm and dry. The thought of being stuck inside with Fungus's terrible stink was just too much. Perhaps Bogweed could help with that, too.

As she walked between the overhanging trees, trailing vines and mud pools, the ground beneath Flora's feet started getting warmer. Here and there, patches of swamp mud had dried and cracked in the heat. Clouds of steam filled the air and a terrible sound met her ears. It was an ear-splitting, screeching, howling sort of noise. It sounded like a wild boar with its foot stuck in a hole.

Bogweed was singing.

As she got closer, Flora spotted Bogweed's fur shoes drying on the end of a branch. She peered through the tall marsh grass and, sure enough, there was her youngest son.

Bogweed was sitting in a pool of hot, bubbling water, singing at the top of his voice.

"Hello, Mother," he said, as he splashed about and poured water over his hair.

Bogweed had discovered the pong pit by accident. One day he had been out trying to catch fish with Fungus when –

**SPLAT!**

A huge dollop of mud flew through the air and hit him right in the face.

As the stinky black mud ran into his eyes and mouth, Bogweed had run around blindly while Fungus had rolled around on the floor howling with laughter. Unable to see where he was going, Bogweed had tripped and stumbled across the rocks and stones until –

**SPLOSH!**

Hot, bubbling water had covered him from head to foot. Bogweed had kicked and splashed for a moment, coughing and spluttering, until he realised the water was shallow enough for him to sit in. Then he had relaxed and let the hot, bubbly water wash off all the mud and dirt. He felt cleaner than he'd ever felt in his life.

It was *wonderful*!

The next day, Bogweed had piled rocks and stones to form a barrier around the spot where the hot water bubbled up into the river. Not only did it make a private little pool for him to lie in, it also helped keep some of the river water out of Slimepool Swamp.

Bogweed loved it.

Fungus called it the pong pit.

Now Flora sat on the edge of the pong pit and dipped her muddy feet into the water. She had to admit it *did* feel nice as the hot water bubbled around her toes. Surely Fungus wouldn't kick up too much of a fuss if he ended up in there.

"I've had an idea," said Flora Mudcrust proudly to her son. "And I need *your* help."

# Chapter Two

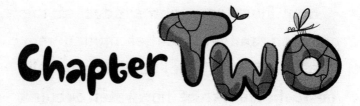

Bogweed was not happy.

His mother's ideas always meant trouble for someone, and that someone was usually him. And as soon as Flora told him what she had in mind, Bogweed knew it was probably her worst idea yet.

"No!" he cried. "I won't do it. I can't do it. It's too dangerous."

"Don't worry," smiled Flora. "It'll be easy. And just think how much better it will be for everyone afterwards."

Bogweed was not convinced. Getting Fungus into the pong pit might make him smell nice, but it would *not* be easy. And it certainly wouldn't make things better for Bogweed. Fungus would be furious. But there was something about the look on his mother's face that told him he didn't have much choice.

"Come on," said Flora. "There's no point in hanging around. You might as well do it now."

"Right now?" spluttered Bogweed. "But I need time to make a plan."

"I'm sure you'll think of something once you get him here," said Flora. "And *I* know how we can do that."

When they got back home, everything was quiet and there was no sign of Fungus or Lowbrow.

"Perhaps they've gone hunting," said Bogweed, hopefully. "Never mind. There's no rush, is there?"

Flora did not answer. Instead, she opened the door of their hut and popped her head in.

The unmistakeable sound of snoring could be heard rumbling from inside. Bogweed's heart sank. Lowbrow and Fungus *were* there after all, fast asleep.

"Well," Flora roared, giving her hands a thunderous clap. "We're home!"

"Oh!" cried Lowbrow, jumping up and bumping his head on the soggy roof. "We were just about to go and see if we could catch a wild boar for our dinner."

"Don't you worry, my dear," said Flora, smiling. "You sit down and put your feet up. Bogweed can go out hunting, can't you, love?"

Bogweed was not very good at hunting and normally made a complete mess of it. But this was all part of his mother's plan.

"Er, of course," he said, struggling to pick up a heavy wooden club and nearly dropping it on his foot. "I'll catch something tasty for us. Don't you worry."

"No way!" said Fungus, yawning and rubbing his eyes. "Bogweed can't go hunting on his own – he can't even catch a cold."

"You go with him, then," said his mother.

"Hunt with Bogstink!" said Fungus. "You must be joking. He'll get us eaten by a bear, or something. I'll go on my own."

"Nonsense," said Flora. "Now off you go. *Both* of you."

Fungus stormed out of the hut and slammed the door behind him. He wasn't happy. Hunting with his father was fine, but Bogweed made it hard work and something always went wrong.

Bogweed didn't look very happy, either, but Flora smiled and gave him a wink as he dragged the heavy wooden club behind him and went out after his brother.

As the door of their hut closed, Bogweed looked around for Fungus. First he needed to take his brother back through the swamp towards the pong pit. But there was no sign of him anywhere. Fungus had disappeared.

Bogweed tried to remember what his father had taught him about tracking animals. He looked down at the muddy ground for telltale footprints.

He was in luck. There were lots of footprints, and some of them were huge. They definitely belonged to Fungus. Bogweed could see the marks that his brother's knuckles had left in the mud as he'd dragged them along behind him. The only problem was there were *hundreds* of footprints, and they all went off in different directions. Fungus could have gone anywhere.

"Oh well," said Bogweed to himself. "At least I tried."

He was just about to go back and tell his mother that her plan would have to wait when Fungus popped his head out from behind a tree.

"Oi! Stinkweed," he shouted. "Are you coming or not?"

Bogweed had opened his mouth to answer when a huge dollop of mud flew through the air and hit him in the face –

**SPLOT!**

Bogweed squealed and dropped the club.

"Ha!" laughed Fungus. "I said you were too much of a wet wimp to go hunting. Why don't you just stay at home?"

That did it. Bogweed was fed up with Fungus teasing him and calling him names. He clenched his fists, screwed up his eyes and let out a loud roar. Then he charged at his brother like a raging bull.

His feet squelched and slipped on the ground as mud splashed onto his legs, but he didn't care. For once, Fungus was going to be sorry. He'd think twice before making fun of him again.

Bogweed moved so quickly that Fungus didn't have the chance to get out of the way and –

**THUD!**

Bogweed ran straight into him.

It felt as though he had run into a tree. Bogweed staggered backwards and fell flat on his back into the soft, swampy mud.

"Urgh!" he said, rubbing his head. He opened his eyes and saw his brother peering down at him with a puzzled look on his face.

"Stop messing about, Bogslime," said Fungus. "Those wild boar aren't going to catch themselves, you know."

# Chapter THREE

Bogweed shook his head and watched as Fungus walked towards the forest in front of the swamp. He was going in the wrong direction!

"Not that way," shouted Bogweed. "Mother says she has just seen wild boar at the other end of the swamp."

Fungus stood still for a moment and frowned.

"What are they doing there?" he asked, scratching his head. "We never catch wild boar at the *other* end of the swamp."

Bogweed had to think quickly. If Fungus grew suspicious, he'd never get him to go anywhere.

"How should I know?" he said. "You're the hunter. Shall we go to the forest instead?"

"No!" cried Fungus. "We'll go where Mother said."

As Fungus stomped back, Bogweed breathed a sigh of relief and smiled to himself. He knew Fungus was frightened of going into the forest, even though he would never admit it to anyone.

Picking up the club, Bogweed hurried to keep up with his brother. Fungus walked quickly, but that wasn't the only thing that made it difficult for Bogweed to keep up. It was the terrible smell.

Whenever Bogweed got too close, his eyes began to water and he couldn't see where he was going. He understood why Flora was so keen for Fungus to have a good soak.

"What's the matter with you?" said Fungus. "You should be enjoying the lovely fresh air, not holding your nose. You really are a wet wimp."

Bogweed ignored him and tried to work out what he was going to do. The closer they got to the pong pit, the more worried he became. His mother clearly hadn't thought this through. How on earth was he supposed to get Fungus in the water? The knuckle-headed numbskull was too big and strong to be forced anywhere. Bogweed would have to use all his brainpower if he was going to come up with a clever plan, and he would have to do it fast.

Bogweed was deep in thought when they reached the edge of the swamp. He was looking over at the tall marsh grass that grew near the pong pit, and walked straight into Fungus. "Oi!" he cried. "Watch what you're doing."

"Shh!" said Fungus, crouching down behind a rock. "There they are."

"What?" said Bogweed.

He peered over the top of the rock and stared in amazement. He often came to the river on his way to the pong pit, but he had never seen wild boar there before. But now, here they were. And not just one – there was a whole family of them.

"Right," said Fungus. "You sneak round behind and send the boar this way. I'll grab one as it runs past. But remember, it's the big one we want."

Bogweed did not like the sound of this one bit. Catching wild boar was not part of the plan. But he couldn't think what else to do.

Dragging the heavy wooden club behind him, Bogweed slowly crept along the edge of the river until he was behind the family of wild boar. Then he leapt out and ran towards them, waving his arms and shouting, "Shoo! Shoo! Go away!"

The smallest boars ran off squealing and snorting, and one of the adults ran with them, but the big male boar didn't move. Bogweed got closer and closer,

still waving and shouting, but the boar didn't budge. At last, Bogweed stopped running and the boar turned its head and stared at him with one beady eye.

The creature slowly lowered its nasty-looking tusks and grunted.

Bogweed dropped the club and ran.

The boar charged after him.

"HELP!" screamed Bogweed, as he raced around a big rock with the boar close behind him.

Bogweed led the beast back to where Fungus was hiding and, as it went past, Fungus jumped onto its back.

"Yah!" he shouted.

Bogweed stopped running and looked around. He had expected the animal to collapse beneath Fungus's weight, but it didn't. It just let out another loud grunt and speeded up. The boar turned and ran back in the other direction, with Fungus still hanging onto its back.

"Stop it!" yelled Fungus, as the wild boar came running towards Bogweed.

"Stop what?" asked Bogweed, looking puzzled.

"The boar. Hit it with your club!"

The boar twisted and turned, jumped and kicked, as it tried to shake the big smelly thing off its back, but Fungus was determined not to let go. He gripped the creature's short fur as tightly as he could.

As the boar came closer, Bogweed picked up the heavy wooden club and lifted it above his head. Just before it reached him, Bogweed swung the club with all his might...

And three things happened –

1. The wild boar stopped suddenly. 2. Fungus went flying through the air. And 3. the club shot out of Bogweed's hands and disappeared into the trees.

The boar let out a satisfied grunt and trotted off to join the rest of its family. The club landed deep in the swamp with a soggy squelch, and there was a loud splash as Fungus disappeared.

# Chapter FOUR

"Aargh!" screamed Fungus. "Get me out of here."

Bogweed ran towards the sound of Fungus's cries and then stared down at him in disbelief. Fungus had landed right in the middle of the pong pit. There he was, splashing around madly in the hot, bubbling water.

Bogweed smiled to himself. Mission accomplished. His mother *would* be pleased.

"What's the matter?" asked Bogweed, trying to hide his smile.

"It's ... it's ... it's ... WET!" screamed Fungus.

"Just relax," said Bogweed. "Keep still. You'll get used to it."

But Fungus would not keep still. "I don't *want* to get used to it," he yelled. "Get me out of here – now!" He started kicking at the rocks around the edge of the pong pit.

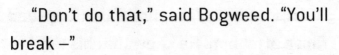

"Don't do that," said Bogweed. "You'll break –"

But it was too late. One of Fungus's fists had already punched through the wall of rocks behind him and the river water that had built up against the barrier was starting to pour in.

"Now look what you've done," said Bogweed.

But Fungus didn't care. One huge foot smashed another hole in the wall and his other foot made it bigger.

Bogweed watched helplessly. "Stop!" he shouted. "You're going to flood the swamp."

Fungus stopped kicking and splashing. He clambered out of the pong pit and glared at his brother. "Just you wait until Mother finds out."

Fungus set off at a run and Bogweed raced after him. He knew that his mother would be happy to hear that Fungus had landed in the pong pit – but he did not think she would be happy to hear about the water that was now pouring into Slimepool Swamp.

As they ran, Bogweed could see that the mud pools were starting to fill up, and the pathways between them were getting very slippery.

"Slow down," shouted Bogweed. "You're going to fall in."

"Shut up, Stinkweed," shouted Fungus. "You can't tell me what to –"

But Fungus didn't get the chance to finish what he was saying. His foot slipped, and he went flying through the air –

**PLOP!**

Fungus landed right in the middle of one of the mud pools.

"Help!" he yelled, waving his arms around.

He kicked and struggled to try and get himself out, but it was no use. The more he moved, the worse it got. He was sinking deeper and deeper into the oozing mud with every movement he made.

"Keep still," shouted Bogweed. He had seen animals get stuck in the mud of Slimepool Swamp. He had seen them kick and struggle as they tried to get out, but they never did. It was almost impossible on your own.

"Help!" cried Fungus, desperately.

Bogweed looked at the thick, dark mud and thought about the day Fungus had pushed him into one of the mud pools for fun. His brother had certainly laughed, but Bogweed remembered how it had felt as the stinking ooze pulled him down. He had hated the sight of mud ever since. Even the thought of it made him shiver and brought him out in goosebumps.

"Aargh," squealed his brother. "I won't tell Mother about how you pushed me into the pong pit, I promise."

But Bogweed wasn't listening. He was remembering how bad the mud had tasted as it got in his mouth. How it had felt as it slowly oozed into his nose and stopped him from breathing. He remembered Chief Hawknose reaching down to rescue him, and how Fungus had cried when he realised how serious it had all been.

Now Fungus's face was sinking beneath the mud, and one hand was waving around desperately in the air trying to grab hold of something.

"Glub," said Fungus.

Someone had to rescue Fungus, and they had to do it now. Bogweed looked around hopefully, but there was no one else. There was only one thing for it. Boldly, he grabbed one of the vines that had wrapped itself around an overhanging tree and tied it around his waist. Taking a deep breath, he stepped off the path and into the mud pool –

**GLOOP!**

Immediately, Bogweed started sinking. He let out a loud scream as mud splashed onto his face. Then something grabbed hold of him. He felt himself being pulled down, deeper and deeper.

It was Fungus.

Bogweed took a deep breath and closed his mouth as the mud slowly crept over his chin.

"Glub," said Fungus, and held on tighter to his brother.

Bogweed held onto the vine as firmly as he could. Slowly, he started to pull the two of them back towards the path. When they reached the side of the mud pool, Bogweed and Fungus dragged themselves out of the thick black gunge. At last, they lay side by side on the path, trying to get their breath back.

Bogweed was exhausted. All he wanted to do was lie there and rest, but he knew there was no time for that. They had to get back to the hut to warn their parents that Slimepool Swamp was flooding.

He got shakily to his feet and started scraping some of the mud off his arms and legs, but it was no use, he was filthy. Not as bad as Fungus, though. His brother looked like a strange creature that had been made completely out of mud.

"Are you all right?" asked Bogweed.

Fungus didn't answer. He just stood there, scratching his head.

"I've just risked my life to rescue you from that mud pool," said Bogweed. "Isn't there something you want to say?"

Fungus looked at him for a moment, then started sniffing.

*Oh no*! thought Bogweed. *He's going to cry*.

But Fungus did not cry. He moved a bit closer to Bogweed and kept on sniffing.

"Ah!" he said, nodding his muddy head.

"What?" said Bogweed.

"You stink," said Fungus, with a muddy grin.

# Chapter FIVE

Fungus and Bogweed ran back to their hut as quickly as they could, but it was hard going. Slimepool Swamp was getting swampier by the minute.

When they finally got there, they stopped and stared in horror. They were too late!

One side of the hut had collapsed completely and Lowbrow was desperately trying to hold up the roof. Muddy water was swirling through the open doorway and they could see their mother standing on a rock, trying to rescue her favourite wooden bowls as they floated past.

"What on earth have you two been up to?" said Flora Mudcrust, when she noticed her sons. "You're filthy."

Bogweed and Fungus looked at each other, but neither knew what to say.

"Well don't just stand there like a couple of dodos," she said. "You can start by helping me off this rock."

While Fungus helped his mother across to the path, Bogweed carried her bowls and tried to rescue a few other bits and pieces. There wasn't much left though, just a soggy, wet roll of mammoth fur and a couple of hunting spears. Everything else had already sunk beneath the muddy water.

As Bogweed passed things to his mother, there was a strange noise behind him. He looked round just in time to see the rest of their hut collapse and sink into the mud. Then, with a final **GLOOP!** the Mudcrust's home disappeared from sight.

Lowbrow looked at his wife miserably, then he sniffed and wiped his dripping nose on the back of his arm.

"It's gone," he said. "I can't believe it. The Mudcrust family home has stood here for years."

"Never mind," said Flora. "It could have been worse."

"Worse!" sniffed Lowbrow. "How could it have been *worse*?"

"At least *we're* all right," said Flora. "We can easily find somewhere else to live."

"But our home is *here*," said Lowbrow.

"Not any more, it's not," said Flora. "It's time for our family to move up in the world. From now on we're going to have a home with a bit of comfort.

"Where are we going to go?" asked Fungus.

"We could stay with the Redwoods," suggested Bogweed. "They've got a big treehouse in the forest."

"I'm not living in a tree," said Lowbrow. "We're not monkeys."

"And *I'm* not living in the forest," said Fungus.

"We'll go and see Chief Hawknose," said Flora. "I'm sure he can help us."

"Bignose!" cried Lowbrow. "I'm not asking that old cheat for help."

"You don't need to," said Flora. "*I'll* ask him."

"But –" began Lowbrow.

"No buts," insisted Flora. "Hawknose is chief of the tribe and it's up to him to find us somewhere else to live."

Lowbrow felt too upset to argue any more. He just nodded his head and set off along the winding path that would take them up the valley towards Icecap Mountain.

Fungus picked up the roll of soggy mammoth fur and hurried after his dad. Bogweed walked behind them with his mother and tried to explain what had happened at the pong pit.

"Never mind," said Flora. "It's a shame Fungus didn't end up any cleaner, but you can't have everything, can you?"

Bogweed was surprised that his mother wasn't angry. In fact, it was just the opposite – she actually seemed *happy* to be leaving their old home behind. It was almost as if this was what she had *wanted* from the very start. Surely she hadn't been *planning* it all along...

The Hawknose family were just settling down for the night when there was a knock at the door.

"Who on earth can this be?" said Chief Hawknose.

"I've no idea," said Fauna.

Their daughter, Mere, went to have a look.

"It's Aunt Flora," said Mere, opening the door to let the Mudcrusts in.

"We're sorry to bother you all so late in the day," said Flora, stepping into the Hawknose's cave, "but we've got nowhere else to go."

Lowbrow reluctantly followed his wife inside. He glared at Chief Hawknose in silence while Flora explained what had happened to their hut.

Bogweed and Fungus stood by the entrance looking uncomfortable. The Hawknose's cave was spotlessly clean, and *they* were covered in mud.

"Come and sit down," said Mere, beckoning them inside. "You must be freezing."

The two brothers squelched across the floor, leaving a trail of mud behind them, and sat down by the fire to dry out. While Fungus stared into the fire, Bogweed looked around in wonder.

It had been a long time since he had last visited the Hawknose's cave, and it was amazing. He could see why his mother liked it so much. They had brightly coloured pictures on the walls, stone shelves to keep things on, and even a big fur rug on the floor.

"We've lost everything," Flora was saying. "And we've got nowhere to live."

"Don't worry," said Fauna. "You can all stay here until we find you somewhere else."

"WHAT?" cried Lowbrow and Chief Hawknose, together.

"We *can't* stay here," said Lowbrow.

"No, they *can't*," agreed Chief Hawknose. He didn't want the Mudcrusts living with him. These were modern times and the world was changing, but the Mudcrusts were so primitive that they still lived in the mud. One look at Bogweed and Fungus was enough to tell him that. They were filthy and they smelt terrible.

"Of *course* they can stay here," said Fauna, scowling at her husband. "It's a huge cave, and there are only three of us."

"But —" said Chief Hawknose.

"No buts," interrupted his wife. "Unless you can think of anywhere else my sister and her family can live."

Chief Hawknose frowned for a moment and scratched his head.

"Well," he said slowly. "There might be another cave a bit higher up the mountain."

"*Another* cave?" said Lowbrow, staring at Chief Hawknose. "You've never said there were *other* caves on Icecap Mountain."

Chief Hawknose went bright red. "I don't think it's very big," he said. "And it will probably need a good clean out."

"I'm sure it will be fine," said Flora quickly. Things were working out even better than she had hoped. A cave of their own – it was a dream come true!

"That's settled then," said Fauna. "You can move in tomorrow."

"Oh," said Flora. "We'll be neighbours – won't that be nice."

"It'll be *lovely*," agreed Fauna. "We'll be able to see so much more of each other."

While Flora carried on chatting to her sister, Bogweed and Fungus fell asleep in front of the fire. But Lowbrow sat on his own in a dark corner, frowning. He didn't think it sounded lovely at all. He still felt miserable about their hut sinking into the mud, and the thought of seeing more of Chief Bignose and his family didn't make him feel any better. There was only one thing for it. Things were going to have to change. And the sooner he became chief, the better...